With
love
to
Paul
and
to
Philip

A PaperStar Book, published in 1998 by The Putnam & Grosset Group,
200 Madison Avenue, New York, NY 10016. PaperStar is a registered
trademark of The Putnam Berkley Group, Inc. The PaperStar
logo is a trademark of The Putnam Berkley Group, Inc.
Originally published in 1995 by Grosset & Dunlap.
Published simultaneously in Canada. Manufactured in China
Library of Congress Cataloging-in-Publication Data
Heller, Ruth, 1924-   Behind the mask : a book about prepositions /
written and illustrated by Ruth Heller.   p.   cm.
Summary: Explores through rhyming text the subject of prepositions and
how they're used.   1. English language—Prepositions—Juvenile literature.
[1. English language—Prepositions.] I. Title.
PE1335.H45   1995   428.2—dc20   95-9535   CIP   AC
ISBN 0-698-11698-4

9   10   8

RUTH HELLER

WORLD OF LANGUAGE

BEHIND THE MASK

A Book About Prepositions

Written and illustrated by

RUTH HELLER

PAPERSTAR

The Putnam & Grosset Group

Of
PREPOSITIONS
have no fear.

They
help to make
directions clear.

beyond
this
green,
reptilian
beast . . .
past its hungry,
gaping
mouth . . .

veer directly . . .

to the south,
toward a place
where mermaids flock
upon,
beside,
and **near** a rock.

One
hundred
twenty
paces
west . . .
the
treasure
lies
inside
this
chest.

PREPOSITIONS
are the best!

They're never alone.
They're always
in phrases . . .

behind

the
masks
and . . .

through the mazes.

They almost always start the phrase . . .

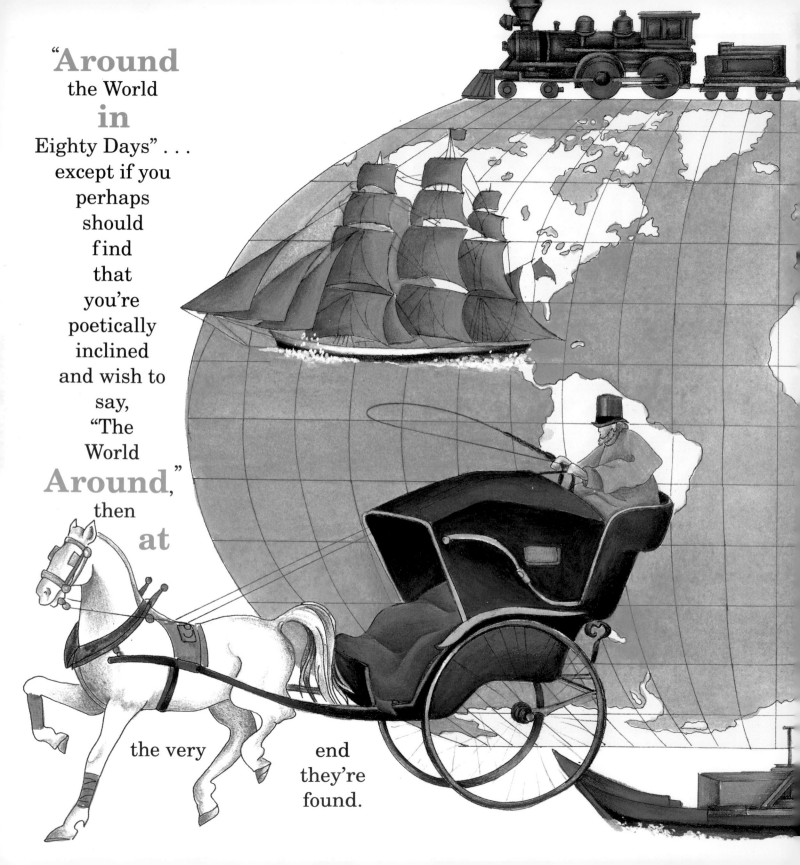

"**Around** the World **in** Eighty Days" . . . except if you perhaps should find that you're poetically inclined and wish to say, "The World **Around**," then **at** the very end they're found.

Of PREPOSITIONS have no fear.

In phrases only they appear.

So if a word **upon** this list **without** a phrase is found . . .

about

above

across

after

against

along

amid

among

around

at

atop

before

behind

below

beneath

beside

besides

between

beyond

but

by
concerning
down
during
except
for
from
in
inside
into
like

near
of
off
on
onto
out
outside
over
past
regarding
since

through
throughout
to toward
under
underneath
until
unto
up upon
with
within
without

as when I say . . .

"Please step inside,
come in,
and
look around."
It's not a
PREPOSITION,
so
take a careful look.
It's
probably an
ADVERB

and is **in**
another
book.

So you will never be confused . . . here are some rules
that can be used.
The cow jumped
over
the
moon.

The
dish ran
away
with the spoon.
PREPOSITIONS tell you where.

They
tell you how . . .

and
when.
Please don't
wake us
until
ten.

Into
means
"to enter,"
and
that's the reason
why . . .
"Step **into** my parlor,"
said
the
spider
to the fly.

But if inside *already* is what you really mean . . .
then . . . eating bread and honey . . .

in
the parlor
is the queen.

Be angry **with** a person, but angry **at** a thing.
I'm angry **with** Jack
and
I'm angry **with** Jill . . .
but,
I'm angrier
still
at
the
pail
and
the
hill.

Between must be said when referring **to** two, and **among** when referring **to** more.

The ten is **between** the king and the queen . . .

and the five is **among** these four.

Say, " different **from**," not "different than."
Find the odd one if you can.

This is a test. . . . Which one is different **from** the rest?

One PREPOSITION is one too many **in** sentences that don't need any.

Where have you been at?